MAXIMUM GIRL UNMASKED

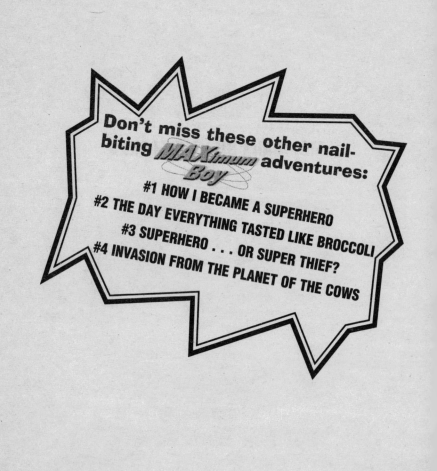

starring in
MAXIMUM GIRL
UNMASKED

BY DAN GREENBURG
ILLUSTRATIONS BY GREG SWEARINGEN

A Little Apple Paperback

SCHOLASTIC INC.
New York   Toronto   London   Auckland   Sydney
Mexico City   New Delhi   Hong Kong   Buenos Aires

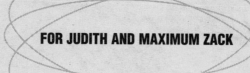

FOR JUDITH AND MAXIMUM ZACK

No part of this publication may be reproduced in whole or in part, or stored in a retrieval system, or transmitted in any form or by any means, electronic, mechanical, photocopying, recording, or otherwise, without written permission of the publisher. For information regarding permission, write to Scholastic Inc., Attention: Permissions Department, 555 Broadway, New York, NY 10012.

ISBN 0-439-21948-5

Text copyright © 2002 by Dan Greenburg.
Illustrations copyright © 2002 by Scholastic Inc.

All rights reserved. Published by Scholastic Inc.

SCHOLASTIC, LITTLE APPLE PAPERBACKS, and associated logos are trademarks and/or registered trademarks of Scholastic Inc.

12 11 10 9 8 7 6 5 4 3   2 3 4 5 6 7 8/0

Printed in the U.S.A.
First Scholastic printing, February 2002

CHAPTER 1

Don't ever let your teenage sister become a superhero. You'll be sorry if you do. *I* sure am. I guess I'd better explain.

My name is Max Silver. I'm eleven. I wear braces and glasses. I live in Chicago. Three years ago, at the Air and Space Museum, I accidentally handled some rocks that had just come back from outer space. Suddenly, I was able to do things that most eleven-year-olds can't. Like fly. And lift freight trains. And punch out supervillains. And hop on one foot for about an hour if I want to.

If I don't use my superpowers, I'm the second-worst athlete in the sixth grade. But if I used them I'd give away my secret identity, and that would put my family in danger. You'd think I could use just a *little* of my superpowers and be just a *little* stronger and faster than the other kids, but that's not how superpowers work. With superpowers it's all or nothing. That's so *unfair*.

I do have a few weaknesses: ragweed, milk products, sweet potatoes, and math. Just *hearing* a math problem is enough to knock me unconscious. Superman had the same problem with kryptonite. I'm the only kid in the sixth grade with a doctor's excuse to get out of math.

Because of my superpowers, the President of the United States sends me on lots of missions to help our country. Like the time an evil scientist named Dr. Zirkon citynapped the island of Manhattan and towed it out to sea. Or the time a supervillain called Ethelred the Unready stole the greatest treasures in the world. Or the time Earth was invaded by evil cattle from the Planet of the Cows.

My teenage sister, Tiffany, got so jealous of all the attention I was getting, she went nuts. When her class took a trip to the Air and Space Museum, she broke into the space rocks exhibit and handled the same radioactive rocks I had. They did give her superpowers. And she did force my mom to make her a uniform like mine. But she's a really lousy superhero. For one thing, she should never be allowed to fly. She's always bumping into stuff like airplanes and the Washington Monument. For another thing, she just isn't cool about having a secret identity.

I'll tell you what I mean.

Today, Monday, she came home after school and said, "Guess what! I'm going to be on, like, the front page of our school newspaper!"

"That's lovely, Tiffany," said my mother. "What did you do?"

"I won the high jump in gym."

"How high did you jump?" I asked. I was beginning to get a really bad feeling.

"Twenty-one feet," she said proudly. "It was so *cool*."

"Twenty-one feet!" I said. "Are you *crazy*?"

"What do you mean?"

"Tiffany, no ordinary human being can high-jump twenty-one feet," I said. "By showing off and using your superpowers, you're going to blow our secret identities."

"Oh, relax, Max," said Tiffany. "Don't get your undies in a knot. Nobody outside Bosco High is ever going to *hear* about this. Besides, the coach wants me on the track team now, and I'm suddenly popular in my school for, like, the first time in *history*. I've even been invited to a big sleepover party this weekend. So it's worth it."

"It is not!"

"Is so!"

"Is not!"

"Is so!"

"Mom, is it OK with you that Tiffany has blown our secret identities and exposed you and Dad to life-threatening danger?"

"Well, Tiffany," said my mom, "Max does have a point. I mean, if the media finds out you're Maximum Girl, then . . ."

"Then *what*?" said Tiffany.

"Then supervillains could kidnap Mom and Dad," I said. "And use them to force us to stop battling the forces of evil. But you're so selfish, all you could think of was showing off for your stupid friends."

"That is so *untrue*," said Tiffany. "I don't even *have* any friends. I was showing off for, like, total *strangers*."

Just then the phone rang. It was the President of the United States.

"Max," he said, "something terrible has happened. You have to come to Washington immediately!"

"What's wrong, sir?" I asked.

"I'm afraid I can't tell you that," he said. "But I'm in terrible trouble, Max. The worst trouble I've ever been in as President. How soon can you be here?"

"I'll ask my mom, sir," I said. "Mom, the President of the United States is in terrible trouble. The worst trouble he's ever been in as President. Can I go to Washington?"

"Did you finish your science homework?" she asked.

"Not really."

"Well then, I'm afraid you can't go to Washington."

"But, Mom, the President is in the worst trouble he's ever been in. He's panicking."

"I am not *panicking*, Max," said the President on the phone. "The President of the United States does not *panic*. I'm just very . . . *concerned*."

"Ask him if this trouble has anything to do with supervillains," said my mom.

"Why?"

"Because trouble with supervillains always takes such a long time," she said. "If there are no supervillains involved, maybe you could go for just a short time."

"Sir," I said into the phone, "Mom says if there are no supervillains involved, maybe I could come for a short time."

"Well, I don't know if there are any supervillains involved, Max," said the President. "I don't *think* there are, anyway."

"Mom, the President doesn't think there are any supervillains involved," I said.

"Well then, I suppose it's OK," said Mom. "But I do want you home in time for dinner. We're having lasagna."

"Tiffany was so helpful during the invasion from the Planet of the Cows," said the President on the phone. "I'd like her to come with you."

"Tiffany," I said, "the President wants you to come to Washington to help him, too."

"I can't," said Tiffany. "Denise, Heather, Ashley, and Kimberly invited me to the mall. We're going shopping for lipstick."

"Tiffany," I said. "Like it or not — and I don't — you're a superhero now. And when your President needs you, it's more important than shopping for stupid *lipstick*."

Tiffany sighed a big sigh.

"OK, *fine*," she said. "I'll come with you to Washington. OK? You satisfied?"

"Don't do me any favors," I said.

CHAPTER 2

Flying to Washington with Tiffany was a real pain. Before we even left Chicago, she bumped into both the Hancock Building and the Sears Tower. I had to keep grabbing her whenever she lost altitude. One time, she got caught in the vacuum behind a passing 747 and almost got her cape sucked into a jet engine.

When we landed on the White House

lawn, Tiffany came down too fast and fell on her butt. She was pretty grouchy till the Marine guards came up to us.

"Excuse me, miss," said the first Marine. He was pretty young-looking. "The public is not permitted on White House grounds. You'll have to leave immediately."

"It's OK," I said. "I'm Maximum Boy and she's with me. The President is expecting us."

"*Sir*, yes, *sir!*" said the Marine. He saluted us. "Sorry to have bothered you, Maximum Boy!"

Suddenly, Tiffany got all weird and flirty with the two Marines.

"Hi. I'm Maximum Girl," she said. She fluttered her eyelashes at them and smiled. "But you can call me Tiffany."

I couldn't believe she was giving them her real name.

"Excuse me, *Maximum Girl*," I said. "I believe the President is expecting us."

I grabbed her roughly by the wrist and dragged her toward the White House entrance.

"Hey," said Tiffany, "let *go*! What are you *doing*?"

"What am *I* doing? What are *you* doing?" I said. " 'Hi, I'm *Max*-i-mum Girl, but *you* can call me *Tiff*-a-ny,' " I mimicked. "Why don't you just wear a big poster on your chest that says 'My secret identity is Tiffany Silver. I live in Chicago with my mom, Rose Silver, and my dad, Sam Silver'? Why don't you just give our address and phone number to the whole entire United States Marine Corps?"

"Is that what you're so bummed about? That I gave my name to those Marines? They were so *cute*."

A Secret Service man with what looked like a hearing aid in his ear came up to us.

"Good afternoon, Maximum Boy, Maxi-

mum Girl," he said. "The President is expecting you."

He took us into the White House and
along a hallway in the West Wing to the
door of the Oval Office. Just before he
opened the door to the Oval Office, he
stopped.

"When was the last time you saw the
President?" he whispered.

"About a week ago," I whispered. "Why?"

"The President is, uh . . . well, he's not
quite himself today," he whispered. "Try not to
act shocked if he looks a little . . . different."

"Is he sick?" I whispered.

"Uh . . . in a way," whispered the Secret
Service guy. "But don't mention it unless *he*
does. OK?"

"OK," I said.

The Secret Service man opened the door, and we went into the Oval Office. Sitting behind the President's desk, wearing a striped tie, a white shirt, and a navy blue blazer with the Presidential crest on the pocket, was . . . a chimpanzee!

CHAPTER 3

"Oh, there you are," said the chimp at the desk. "Thanks for getting here so quickly, kids. How are your mom and dad?"

"Oh . . . uh . . . well, they're, you know, fine," I said.

"Good, good. Glad to hear it," said the chimpanzee. He suddenly jumped up on the desk, shouted "EEEP! EEEP! EEEP!" and then climbed back into the chair.

Tiffany and I looked at each other, then at the chimpanzee. I had never seen a talking chimp before, except in the movies.

"What are you staring at?" said the chimp. He sounded irritated.

"Nothing," I said.

"We've just never seen a talking chimp before," said Tiffany. "Except in the movies, of course. How are you doing that?"

"How am I doing *what*?" asked the chimp.

"Making it look like you're talking?" I said.

The chimp got really mad at that.

"I'm not making it *look* like I'm talking, I *am* talking," said the chimp. "I'm not some stupid chimp, I'm the President of the United States. I'm the leader of the free world!"

"Oh," I said. "Sorry, sir. You just look kind of different is all."

"Of *course* I look different," said the chimp. "Somebody changed me into a stupid chimpanzee. That's why I called you here. I need help. I have to go on TV on Thursday night and give a speech to the American people. How seriously will they take that speech if it's given by a chimpanzee?"

"Probably not all that seriously," I said.

"Exactly," he said. He hit a button on his intercom.

"Yes, Mr. President?" said the voice on the intercom.

"Did you get me the item I asked you for?" he asked.

"Yes, sir," said the voice on the intercom.

"Can you send the item in to me now?"

"Right away, sir," said the voice.

A moment later, the door of the Oval Office opened. A Marine came in. He was carrying a big bunch of bananas on a stalk. The President snatched the bananas out of his hands.

"Thank you, Corporal," said the President.

"*Sir*, yes, *sir!*" said the Marine. He saluted the President and left.

The President ripped two bananas off the stalk. He stuffed them into his mouth, skin and all. He chewed them up and swallowed them.

"There, that's better," he said. "Now then, where were we?"

"You were saying that the American people wouldn't take your speech as seriously if it were given by a chimpanzee," said Tiffany.

"Right," said the President. "So I'm giving the two of you an important job: Find out who or what turned me into a chimp, and then reverse it before Thursday night. You think you can handle that?"

"Well, I don't know, sir," I said. "It depends on — "

"We can do it, sir!" said Tiffany. "You know our motto: The difficult we do immediately. The impossible takes a little longer."

I glared at Tiffany. She stuck her tongue out at me.

"Isn't that the motto of the Marines?" asked the President.

"The Marines . . . copied it from *us*, sir," said Tiffany.

Just then, the President's chief of staff came into the Oval Office. He looked really worried.

"Excuse me, sir," said the chief of staff. "But it seems we have something of a problem."

"What is it?" said the President.

"Sir, the Russian delegation is here for the meeting about the new space station," said the chief of staff. "In the confusion over your . . . change, we forgot to cancel it."

"I see," said the President. "Can you try to reschedule the meeting for another day?"

"Sir, I tried," said the chief of staff. "I told them you were sick and wanted to reschedule. They found that insulting. They threatened to go right back to Russia unless you had the meeting now, as planned."

"I see," said the President. "All right then, show them in."

"But sir, in your present condition . . ."

"We can't have them going back to Russia, now can we?"

"No, sir, but — "

"Don't worry about me," said the President. "Once they get used to my appearance, the meeting will go fine. Show them in."

"Very well, sir. Whatever you say."

The chief of staff left the Oval Office.

"Sir," I said, "maybe this isn't such a good idea. It's not only your appearance. It's also your behavior."

"Behavior? *What* behavior?" said the President. He ripped two more bananas off the stalk and stuffed them into his mouth, skin and all.

The chief of staff came back in. With him were three Russians in uniform, two men and a woman. They had medals all over their chests. With them was a tall, skinny man in a black suit. He had dark pouches under his eyes and looked sad.

"Mr. President," said the chief of staff, "may I present General Plotzsky, General Snotsky, and General Slobotsky. And this," said the chief of staff, pointing to the sad-looking man, "is their interpreter, Mr. Stinkevitch."

Everybody stared at the President. Then the generals said something in Russian.

"Generals weesh to know," said the interpreter, "why you put stinking cheemp een sportycoat and seating heem behind desk of President?"

"I am not a stinking chimp," said the President, a little hurt. "I'm the President of the United States. The leader of the free world. And I welcome you to the White House."

The President stuck out his hand to shake. The generals backed away from it and all started speaking at once.

"Generals say ha-ha-ha, fonny joke," said the interpreter. "But they coming to talk about new space station weeth President, not weeth Bonzo the stinking Cheemp."

"He really *is* the President, not Bonzo the stinking Chimp," I said. "Trust me."

"And who *you* are?" asked the interpreter.

"I'm Maximum Boy," I said, "and this is Maximum Girl."

The interpreter translated for the generals.

"Generals osking eef you de same Moximum Boy who get back stolen painting of Mona Lisa and stolen island of Monhotton."

"I am," I said proudly. I had no idea people knew about me as far away as Russia.

The interpreter translated again for the generals, then turned back to me.

"Generals say Moximum Boy would not lie. Eef Moximum Boy say stinking cheemp ees President, then they meet weeth stinking cheemp."

"What about *me*?" said Tiffany. "*I* say the stinking chimp is the President, *too*."

"Watch it," said the President.

"Sorry, sir," said Tiffany.

"Who *you* are?" asked the interpreter.

"She's Maximum Girl," I said. "She's a superhero, too."

"I'm just as good as Maximum Boy, only taller," said Tiffany.

The interpreter translated again for the generals.

"Generals say meeting about new space station begins," said the interpreter.

The generals all took their seats.

"Excellent," said the President. "Well now, let's talk about the new space station that Russia would like to build with the United States. We may be willing to EEP EEP pay most of the cost, if the Russians agree to EEP EEP, CHUKKA CHUKKA."

Everybody was absolutely quiet.

"Please," said the interpreter. "What means 'eep eep, chukka chukka'?"

I looked nervously at the President.

"What I think the President is trying to say," said the chief of staff, "is that —"

"Please, George," said the President. "Don't put words in my mouth. I can speak for myself."

"Sorry, sir," said the chief of staff.

"What I'm trying to say," said the President, "is that the United States may be willing to pay most of the cost of the new space station. But in return, we want the Russians to EEP EEP, OOGA OOGA, BRAAACK!"

At that, the President grabbed the rest of the bananas. He scampered up the draperies and leaped to the chandelier. He hung by one arm from the chandelier, stuffing bananas into his mouth and chattering.

The generals said something very loud in Russian and stood up.

"Generals say meeting weeth stinking cheemp ees over," said the interpreter. He looked sadder than ever. I thought he might burst into tears any second. "Generals say thees meeting ees terrible insult. Generals

so upset they go back to Russia now and refuse to eat at Moscow McDonald's."

The generals walked angrily to the door of the Oval Office.

"Hang on a second," I called. "I'd just like to say something here."

The generals stopped and turned to look at me.

"I just wanted to tell you that the President isn't himself today," I said. "He's really very sick. He would have canceled today's meeting, but he didn't want to insult you. He begs you to forgive him."

The interpreter translated. The generals talked. The interpreter turned back to me.

"Generals say you nice young man, Maximum Boy. Generals say maybe they don't go back to Russia and refuse to eat at Moscow McDonald's if *you* meet weeth them."

"Well," I said, "sure. If it's OK with the President, I mean."

I looked up at the President to get a sign from him whether it was OK to meet with the Russians or not. The President had finished eating all of his bananas. He had taken off all his clothes and was busy picking bugs out of his fur.

"The President says fine," I said.

CHAPTER 4

Tiffany stayed in the Oval Office to talk the President down out of the chandelier and take care of him. I went to another office with the generals and the interpreter to talk about space stations.

Because I don't know anything about space stations, I was a little worried to be deciding stuff with the generals. But after a while I sort of got the hang of it. The generals agreed that if we paid for most of the space station, American tourists could visit whenever they wanted. They could get astronaut autographs and fool around with the scientific equipment. The Russians agreed not to flush space toilets when the space station was flying over the United States.

When the Russian generals left, I went back to the Oval Office. Tiffany and the chief of staff had gotten the President calmed down a little.

"How did the meeting with the generals go?" asked the President. He was lying on the sofa. He had his suit on again. Tiffany was scratching him behind the ears.

"Pretty well, sir," I said. "I think we have a basic agreement."

"Your fellow Americans can't thank you enough, Maximum Boy," said the President. "I'll tell them about you on TV on Thursday. Assuming I'm no longer a chimp by then, I mean."

"Oooo! Oooo!" said Tiffany. "I have just had, like, the best idea of how the President could do his speech on TV, even if he's still a chimp. You want to hear my idea?"

"What is it?" I asked.

"OK," said Tiffany. "I get the President a makeover by a really cool cosmetics company, OK? Shave him all over, put on lots of makeup and a really cool suit. Nobody will ever know he's a chimpanzee. Maybe they'd even give *me* a makeover while they're at it. Is that a cool idea or what?"

"Frankly, I don't care for it," said the President.

"Frankly, neither do I," I said.

"I'll bet you would have liked it if *Max* had thought of it," said Tiffany.

"Look, sir," I said. "Let's try to figure out how you got to be this way. That's our only hope of getting you back to normal for Thursday."

"Well," said the President, "it happened in my private elevator, going down to the White House garage."

"The one with the minibar?" I asked.

"Right," said the President. "I entered that elevator as a man and left it as a chimpanzee."

"Did you meet anyone suspicious in the elevator?" Tiffany asked.

"How could I have met somebody suspicious in my own private elevator?" said the President.

"I don't know," she said. "Well, did any-thing happen that was at all, like, suspi-cious while you were in the elevator?"

"Now that you mention it, yes," said the President. "I did feel a strange, tingling sen-sation. That must have been when it hap-pened."

"Can I inspect your private elevator?" I asked.

"Of course," said the President.

I went into the President's elevator. Once I turned on my X-ray vision, it didn't take long to find what I was looking for. I discovered a strange device in the ceiling of the elevator. A tiny camera and some kind of ray-producing machine.

I showed it to the White House security people. They didn't have a clue what it was.

"We don't have a clue what this is," they told me.

Could this have been what turned the President into a chimpanzee? If so, how had it worked? More important, who was behind it?

While I was turning these questions over in my mind, an envelope was delivered to the Oval Office. It was addressed to the President. He handed it to me.

I ripped open the envelope. Inside was a note written with a big red crayon in capital letters. I read it out loud:

IF YOU EVER WANT TO GET YOUR HUMAN BODY BACK AGAIN, BRING 100 MILLION DOLLARS

IN SMALL BILLS TO THE TOP OF THE
EMPIRE STATE BUILDING WEDNESDAY
AT 8:30 P.M. COME ALONE, OR RE-
MAIN A MONKEY FOREVER.

"Let me see that," said the President.

I handed him the letter. He read it. Then he ate it.

"So what do you think about the letter, sir?" Tiffany asked.

"Didn't have much taste," said the President. "Maybe if it had a little salt . . ."

"No," I said. "She meant what do you think about what it said? About paying a hundred million dollars to get your human body back?"

"Well, it does seem a little expensive," said the President. "But maybe that's what it costs these days to get human bodies back. Anybody know if that's about what they're charging? No? Maybe we ought to shop around for a better price."

"Sir," I said, "having your body switched with a chimp doesn't happen all that often. In fact, I don't think it's *ever* happened before. So you can't shop around for a better price."

"I suppose you're right," said the President. "OK, let's give them the hundred million. What the heck. We've got a lot of money here. Might as well spend it."

"Before you do that, sir," I said, "why don't you let me and Maximum Girl see what we can dig up?"

"Sure," said the President. "Why not? But remember, we only have two days left before Wednesday. If I don't pay them the money, I have to remain a chimp forever."

CHAPTER 5

My friend Tortoise Man lives in an old VW Microbus by the river, not far from the White House. He's a semiretired superhero. He's older than my dad and he's overweight and bald, but he's really nice. Also, he knows practically all the supervillains in the world. I took Tiffany to see him. I thought he might be able to help us.

I told him about the President being a

chimp and about the ransom note demanding a hundred million dollars.

"Turned the President into a chimp, did they?" said Tortoise Man. "How do you suppose they did that?"

"It happened in the President's private elevator," said Tiffany. "I found a tiny camera and this, like, ray-producing thing in the ceiling of the elevator that —"

"*You* found the camera and the ray-producing thing?" I said. "You weren't even there. *I* found it."

"What's the difference who found it?" said Tiffany. "It was found, OK? And it looks like a ray came out of that thing and turned the President into a chimp."

"How they probably did it," said Tortoise Man, "is somebody had a chimp in another location. They focused the beam on the chimp at one end and on the President at the other. Then they reversed the signals."

"They teleported the chimp's body to the White House and the President's body to where they had the chimp," I said.

"Exactly," said Tortoise Man.

"So, somewhere there's somebody who looks like the President of the United States, but with the brain of a chimp," I said. I turned to my sister. "Tiffany, are you thinking what *I'm* thinking?"

"Only if you're thinking of ordering out for pizza," she said.

"No, I mean who do we know who does experiments like that?"

Tiffany stared at me, clueless.

"Dr. Cubic Zirkon," I said. "The evil scientist who citynapped Manhattan? The one who turned into a duck-billed platypus when an experiment he was doing went terribly wrong?"

"Oh, yeah, him," said Tiffany.

"Unless I'm mistaken," said Tortoise Man, "when Zirkon stole Manhattan, there was also a ransom note."

"So it's the same guy," said Tiffany. "Now what?"

"Now," I said, "we need to drop in on Dr. Zirkon. Tortoise Man, do you know where his hideout is?"

Tortoise Man took out a worn copy of *The Directory of Archvillains and Evildoers*. He riffled through the pages.

"Darn!" he said. "This says Zirkon moved his hideout and left no forwarding address."

"Hey, what time is it?" Tiffany asked.

"Almost six o'clock," I said. "Why?"

"Well, like, I have all this French home-

work?" she said. "Plus which, if we're late for dinner, Mom is going to really, you know, kill us?"

Tiffany was right. If we were late for dinner, Mom would go ballistic. So we flew back to Chicago. We still had one more day to decide whether the President should keep his date with Dr. Zirkon on Wednesday night at the top of the Empire State Building.

CHAPTER 6

The next day, Tuesday, Tiffany came home from school and seemed really pumped.

"How cool is *this*?" she said. "A real reporter saw my picture in the school paper. He wants to interview me for a *real* newspaper!"

"I don't *believe* this!" I said. "After I told you how dangerous it would be if you ever blew our secret identities? Where's this reporter from?"

"I don't really remember, but his name is Pratt or Platt or something like that."

"Was it Blatt?" I asked. "Warren Blatt of the *International Enquirer*?"

"Yeah, that's it," said Tiffany. "Why? Do you know him?"

I felt like I was going to explode.

"Warren Blatt wants to do a story on you?" I shouted. "Warren Blatt is the sleaziest reporter in the world! Warren Blatt practically ruined my friend Tortoise Man!"

"How?"

"How? By giving away his secret identity. By giving away all his secrets. You can't talk to him, Tiffany!"

"OK, OK," she said. "So I won't talk to him."

The front doorbell rang. Mom went to see who was there.

"Tiffany?" called Mom from the other end of the apartment. "Someone is here to see you!"

"Who is it?" called Tiffany.

"A gentleman named Warren Blatt!" called my mom.

"Tiffany's not here!" I shouted.

Warren Blatt walked into the apartment.

"Hello, Tiffany," said Blatt. Then he turned to me. "I thought she wasn't here."

"Oh, well, she wasn't," I said. "But then she was. She must have come back when I wasn't looking."

"How could she have come back?" said Blatt. "I was at the door."

"Maybe through the window?" I said.

"Listen, I hate to be rude, but we were actually on our way out. We have an appointment."

Blatt was now staring at me and frowning.

"Who are you, kid, her brother?" he asked.

"Uh, yeah. Why?"

"There's something very familiar looking about you," he said, studying my face. "Have we ever met before?"

Oh, boy. He'd better not remember how many times he's met me as Maximum Boy. Of course, all those times I was wearing my Maximum Boy uniform and my mask.

"I've never met you before," I said.

He was still staring at me, frowning.

"Listen, Mr. Blatt," said Tiffany. "You didn't tell me you were coming. My brother and I have plans. So I'm afraid you'll have to, you know, like, leave."

"Then we'll do this some other time?" Blatt asked.

"No way," she said.

"You'll be sorry, sis," said Blatt. He looked mad. On his way out he turned to me. "I know we've met before," he said. "I can't remember where, kid, but if I think about it hard enough, it'll come to me."

That really gave me the creeps. If Blatt ever figured out where he'd met me, my face and my real name would be on the cover of the next *International Enquirer.*

As soon as Blatt left, the phone rang. Tiffany answered. It was the President.

"How are you feeling, sir?" asked Tiffany.

"Oh, you know. About the same," said the President.

"Are you still a chimp?" she asked.

"I am," said the President. "Have you kids figured out how to help me yet?"

"Just a minute, sir," said Tiffany. "Max," she whispered, "have we figured out how to help him yet?"

I took the phone from Tiffany.

"Not yet, sir," I said. "But we did figure out who did this — Dr. Zirkon, the mad scientist who citynapped Manhattan. I think you should keep your appointment with him at the top of the Empire State Building. Maximum Girl and I will be there, too. And we'll have a little surprise for him."

"Good," said the President. "What kind of surprise?"

"That's a surprise, sir," I said. "If we told you, it wouldn't be a surprise, now would it?"

CHAPTER 7

Wednesday morning. Tiffany and I took the bus to school. As we rode, I worried. Tonight, the President would deliver a hundred million dollars to the top of the Empire State Building to get his human body back. We had to be there, too, and not be seen. We had to make sure the President got into his right body, we had to save the money, and we had to capture Dr. Zirkon. Could we do all that, plus our homework, and still be in bed by our bedtimes?

We got off the bus in front of school. It was about ten minutes before Tiffany's school started, fifteen minutes before mine. The high school and junior high were in the same building. About fifty kids were standing outside the front entrance. There was Charlie Sparks, my best friend. She's the only kid in the world who knows I'm Maximum Boy. She knows about Tiffany, too. She's real little, but she isn't afraid of anybody.

There was Roland Shlotzky. He's not a bad kid, but I have to admit he's kind of geeky. Before I got my superpowers, I was either the slowest kid in class or the second slowest, depending on whether Roland Shlotzky was in school that day.

There was Trevor Fartmeister, the class

bully. He's so tough, nobody has even dared to make a joke about his name. He's two years older than me, but he's in my grade because he flunked twice. He's got a red buzz cut and half his left ear is missing. I heard a kid even bigger than Trevor bit it off in a fight. I heard Trevor bit off the other kid's nose.

Nearby was a bunch of girls in Tiffany's class — Denise, Heather, Ashley, Kimberly, and a few whose names I didn't know. As soon as they saw her, they came rushing over to her.

"Look at them, Max," said Charlie. "Before Monday, they hardly knew she was alive. Now they're falling all over themselves just to talk to her."

"Yeah," I said. "Amazing, isn't it?"

"Imagine how popular she'd be if they

knew she was Maximum Girl," Charlie whispered.

"*Sssssshhh!*" I said. "Let's just hope they never find out."

Just then, Trevor Fartmeister caught sight of me.

"Hey, Silver!" he called. "Is that your head, or is that a giant fungus growing out of your neck?"

Roland Shlotzky giggled. That made me mad. Fartmeister bullies Shlotzky as much as he does me. You'd think Shlotzky wouldn't laugh when Fartmeister picks on somebody else. Maybe he's just relieved it's not him.

"Hey, Silver!" yelled Fartmeister. "What did you bring me for lunch?"

Because of my food allergies, Mom always makes me a special lunch to bring to school. Sometimes Fartmeister takes it just to humiliate me. I could crush him like a cockroach, but I won't. I can't let anybody see my superpowers or I'll blow my secret identity.

"Hey, Silver, I'm *talking* to you!" yelled Fartmeister. "What am I having for lunch today?" He walked over to me and grabbed the paper bag with my lunch. I couldn't stand the idea of Mom's cooking being eaten by a pig like Fartmeister.

"Give that back," I said.

"Make me," said Fartmeister.

"Don't push me or I might," I said.

"Don't *push* you?" said Fartmeister. "Oh, I would *never* do *that*. I would never *push* you."

Fartmeister pushed me so hard I fell onto the sidewalk. Everybody stopped talking to watch what was happening, even

Tiffany's friends. I got up and slapped the dirt off my hands. I was really embarrassed, but I couldn't really do anything about it. Or could I? Even kids without superpowers sometimes strike back at bullies. One well-placed punch and I could make Fartmeister's nose bleed like Old Faithful.

Just then, a black van pulled up, and Warren Blatt hopped out of it. Oh, no! I couldn't punch Fartmeister now or Blatt would realize I was Maximum Boy.

"I just pushed you, Silver," said Fartmeister. "What are you going to do about it?"

"Fartmeister," called Tiffany, "you leave my brother alone!"

"What's the matter, can't your baby brother fight his own battles?" asked Fartmeister.

Everybody was watching us now, including Blatt. Weren't grown-ups supposed to stop bullies from picking on smaller kids? Fartmeister turned back to me.

"What are you going to *do* about it?" Fartmeister taunted. He pushed me again.

"I said leave my brother alone!" called Tiffany.

Fartmeister grabbed me and pinned my arms behind my back. I could have broken his grip easily, but I didn't dare risk it.

"Shlotzky, pull down Silver's pants!" said Fartmeister.

"Don't do it, Shlotzky!" I said.

"Pull them down *now*, Shlotzsky!" shouted Fartmeister.

Shlotzky pulled down my pants. Everybody could see my underpants. The girls screamed with laughter. I would never forgive Shlotzky for this.

Tiffany had had enough. She flew thirty feet through the air and landed with her head in Fartmeister's belly. You could hear the air whoosh out of him.

Everybody cheered. They couldn't believe what they'd just seen. Neither could I. There was a sudden flash. I turned around. Blatt had his camera out and was taking photo after photo. I realized Tiffany had probably just blown her cover in front of everybody, including Blatt, but in that moment I didn't care.

Tiffany yanked down Fartmeister's baggy jeans. He was wearing Powerpuff Girls underpants. The kids laughed so hard, tears came out of their eyes. Fartmeister was desperately trying to pull his jeans up again. I figured, what the heck? I ripped his jeans to pieces and threw them in the school yard. Then I yanked down his Powerpuff Girls underpants so everybody could see his fat white butt.

"Well, Tiffany," said Blatt, "now I know why you can jump so high. Your secret is out, sis! 'MAXIMUM GIRL UNMASKED!' What a story this is going to make!"

CHAPTER 8

The good news was that Trevor Fart-meister had been humiliated in front of the entire school. He had to walk all the way home without any pants. His days as a bully were over.

The bad news was that about fifty kids at both our schools now knew that Tiffany was Maximum Girl. Kids were going ape over her, crowding around her, asking for her autograph, acting like she was a rock star instead of what she was — a teenage girl who'd handled rocks from space at the Air and Space Museum.

"Sorry I had to blow my cover," said Tiffany, when I was able to drag her away from her fans. "I just couldn't stand to see that jerk Fartmeister make a fool of you."

"Thanks for coming to my defense, Tiff," I said. "But we've got a big problem now."

"Blatt," said Tiffany. "I know."

"Unless we stop him," I said, "your secret is going to be front page news in tomorrow's *International Enquirer*."

"What can we do?"

"I don't know," I said. "Maybe Tortoise Man can think of something."

It was eight-thirty A.M. The bell rang. The other kids went into school. But we had

to do something about Tiffany's unmasking, even if it made us late. I called Tortoise Man from a pay phone near school and told him what happened.

"Wow," said Tortoise Man. "You sure don't want that jerk Blatt giving Tiffany's secret identity to the whole world tomorrow."

"It would be terrible," I said. "Our mom and dad would really be in danger."

"You'd probably have to move out of Chicago to someplace where you won't be recognized," said Tortoise Man.

I turned to Tiffany. "Tortoise Man says we might have to move someplace we won't be recognized," I said.

"Like where?" Tiffany asked.

"Like where?" I said into the phone.

"Like Lapland," said Tortoise Man.

"Like Lapland," I said to Tiffany.

"But I've just made all these friends in *Chicago*," she said. "It isn't *fair*."

"Isn't it very cold in Lapland?" I asked.

"Depends on how drafty your igloo is," said Tortoise Man.

"Look," I said into the phone, "isn't

there any way we can stop Blatt from printing that story?"

"The press can print whatever it
wants," said Tortoise Man. "There's nothing
I can think of that might convince him not
to run the story. Unless . . ."

"Unless what?"

"When you were at the League of Superheroes," said Tortoise Man, "did you ever
meet a guy named Pete Delete?"

"I don't think so," I said. "Is he a superhero?"

"No, but he likes to hang out with
them," said Tortoise Man. "He's kind of a
superhero groupie. And he helps them. If
anyone learns a superhero's secret identity, Pete Delete can erase that person's
mind."

"You're kidding me!" I said. "Could he

erase Blatt's so he won't remember Tiffany is Maximum Girl?"

"What?" said Tiffany.

"Hang on a minute, Tiffany," I said.

"He could," said Tortoise Man. "But he may not want to."

"Why not?"

"Well, Delete's a little . . . weird. He likes superheroes but he's jealous of them. And he thinks nobody appreciates him. But what the heck — you might as well give it a shot."

CHAPTER 9

Pete Delete lived in a tiny basement apartment in Baltimore near the inner harbor. It took me and Tiffany about half an hour to get there. It would have taken less time than that, but Tiffany broke a fingernail flying over Indianapolis and insisted on landing and finding a store that sold nail glue.

Delete didn't let us into his apartment.

He opened his door and made us stand in the hall while we talked to him. The hall smelled like cat pee.

"Why should I help you?" he asked. "Give me nine good reasons."

Delete was a ratlike little guy in a dirty bathrobe and bunny slippers. He had yellow teeth and dirty fingernails. He needed a shave, a shower, and some mouthwash.

"OK," I said. "Reason number one: Unless you help us, the *International Enquirer* is going to print a front-page story tomorrow that says my sister here is Maximum Girl."

"And *is* she Maximum Girl?"

"Well, yeah."

"So what's the problem?"

"Are you kidding me?" said Tiffany. "If my secret identity is revealed, our parents could be kidnapped and tortured. We'd have to move to, like, *Lapland* and live in an *igloo*."

Delete laughed. It was not a nice laugh.

"You superheroes are all alike," he said. "Only thinking of yourselves. Why should *I* care if you live in an igloo? Do you see how I live here in this miserable little apartment? It's *freezing* in here. It's forty *degrees* in here. Do you even *care*?"

The air coming out of Delete's apartment *was* awfully cold.

"Why is it forty degrees in your apartment?" I asked. "Outside it's around *eighty*."

"Why? I'll tell you why. *Because I can't turn down my stupid air conditioner!*" shouted Delete. He calmed down. "OK," he said. "I'll allow that reason to count. But I asked for nine. Give me eight more."

"Look, we don't have time to think up

eight more reasons," I said. "I'll make you a deal, Delete. If you come with us now to Blatt's office and erase his memory, I'll fix your air conditioner. Fixing electric appliances happens to be one of my superpowers."

Delete thought that over.

"Fix my air conditioner *and* my toaster oven and you got yourself a deal," he said.

We flew Delete to Washington. By the time we got to the offices of the *International Enquirer* it was ten-thirty. Just ten hours till our appointment at the Empire State Building.

The *International Enquirer*'s offices looked about a hundred years old. The windows were so dirty you couldn't believe they'd ever been clean, even when they were new. Plaster was peeling off the high ceiling. You couldn't tell what color the walls were supposed to be. The whole place stank of old cigarette smoke.

Delete was carrying a black box fitted with toggle switches and glowing buttons — the Mind-Eraser.

"Delete," I said. "If you can invent a machine to erase people's minds, why can't you fix an air conditioner?"

"Because to fix an air conditioner," said Delete, "I'd have to read the *instruction* manual."

I sort of knew what he meant. I didn't like reading instruction manuals, either.

All around us, reporters were writing stories on computers. I checked the headlines on their screens. One said, IDENTICAL TWINS BORN THIRTY YEARS APART! Another said, MAN KEEPS SIXTY-POUND COCKROACH AS PET, WALKS IT ON LEASH! Another said, I MARRIED BIGFOOT!

Nobody seemed to notice that two superheroes in costume and a guy in a filthy bathrobe and bunny slippers were walking through their offices.

We finally found Blatt. He was typing out a story with two fingers on an old manual typewriter. His sleeves were rolled up. A cigarette dangled out of his mouth.

"Well, well, well," said Blatt, looking up. "This *is* a surprise. Tiffany Silver — also known as Maximum Girl — and her brother, Max, and some jerk in a bathrobe and bunny slippers. If you've come all the way to Washington to try and talk me out of running that story on you, it's too late." He pointed to a pile of typed paper beside his

typewriter. "I'm just finishing it up now."

"We haven't come to talk you out of anything," said Delete. "We've come to play you a tape."

"What's on the tape?" asked Blatt.

"A story so hot it will melt the keys on your typewriter," said Delete. "You want to hear?"

Blatt laughed. "Sure, why not?" he said.

Delete put the black box down on the desk next to Blatt. He pressed two glowing buttons on the black box and threw a toggle switch. A strobe light flashed. A sound like a car alarm came from the black box. Blatt twitched, then his head glowed green. Smoke curled out of his ears. The black box shut off.

Blatt looked dazed. He shook his head

like a wet dog. He turned to us and frowned.

"Yes?" he said. "Can I help you folks?"

Tiffany whooped with joy. I gave Delete a high five and grabbed Blatt's story before he noticed.

CHAPTER 10

We still had some unfinished business. Although Blatt's memory of this morning's events had been wiped clean by the Mind-Eraser, about fifty kids at school still knew Tiffany's secret identity.

So we flew Delete and his black box to school. Under my direction, he wiped out the memories of all the kids who'd seen Tiffany use her superpowers.

That made Tiffany sad, because afterward they didn't seem too eager to be her friends. It also made *me* sad, because it meant that now nobody would remember seeing Fartmeister get his pants pulled down. Which meant he was free to keep being a bully and a pain in the butt.

Well, we couldn't afford to think about that now. What we had to think about was our appointment that night at the Empire State Building. We flew Delete to Baltimore and then went back to Chicago to our parents.

"Max! Tiffany!" said Mom. "Your father and I have been worried *sick* about you! Do you have any idea what time it is?"

"Almost four-thirty," I said.

"You're an hour late getting home from school. Where were you?"

"Well, Mom," I said, "first we had to go to Baltimore to see a guy named Pete Delete. Then we had to take him to Washington to erase Warren Blatt's mind. Then we had to take him to school to erase the minds of all the kids who saw Tiffany's superpowers. Right after dinner we have to go to New York to capture Dr. Zirkon and help the President get his human body back."

"Well, you kids may be superheroes," said Mom, "but you still have to help around the house. Before you capture any more supervillains or get any Presidents' bodies back, you're going to set the table, wash the dishes, take out the garbage, and do at least an hour of homework. Is that understood?"

"Yes, Mom," I said.

"Yes, Mom," said Tiffany.

"And what time will this business in New York with the President be over?"

"Well, that's hard to say," I said. "It's supposed to start at eight-thirty, so it could be over as early as nine o'clock."

"If supervillains are involved," said Mom, "you know that always adds an hour. I won't have you staying out past ten o'clock on a school night, young man."

"But, Mom — "

"Don't 'but Mom' me, Max. You don't have time to both capture Dr. Zirkon and get the President's body back. So choose one or the other, or you kids are not leaving this house."

"Dad!" I called. "Mom isn't letting us triumph over evil!"

Dad came into the kitchen in his painter's smock. He's a professional artist, and he's been working on a big oil painting on an easel in the living room. He was wiping his hands on a rag that smelled like turpentine.

"Now, Rose, what's all this about your not letting the kids triumph over evil?" he asked.

"Sam, they know the rules. Bedtime on school nights is nine-thirty for Max, ten for Tiffany. They don't have time tonight to both capture Dr. Zirkon and get the President's body back. I told them they could choose one or the other, but not both."

"Now, Rose," said Dad gently. "*You* know they can't really do just one of those things and not the other. Don't you, dear?"

Mom sighed. "Oh, of course I know that, Sam," she said. "I just get so darned frustrated when they stay out so late on missions that they can't get up in the morning."

Mom frowned at us, then shook her head and sighed.

"All right then," she said. "Go ahead and triumph over evil. But if you see it's getting on toward nine-thirty and you're not quite finished, bring the unfinished part home and do it here."

"You mean like finish tying up Dr. Zirkon in the living room?" I said.

"We'll even help," said Mom.

CHAPTER 11

It was eight-twenty-five P.M. at the top of the Empire State Building. There was nobody in sight. The wind whistled around the corners of the building and tugged at the bricks. A hundred and two stories below, cars and taxis looked like tiny colored beetles.

A chimpanzee in a suit and tie stepped

out onto the balcony of the hundred-and-second floor and looked around. The chimp checked his watch and waited.

"Mr. President," I whispered.

The chimp looked up.

"Maximum Boy, Maximum Girl — thank heavens you're here!" said the President. "I was getting worried."

"Sir, the ransom note said you had to come *alone*," I whispered. "So I'm going to hide right around the corner of the building there. Dr. Zirkon should be here any minute. Tiffany will go now to get the ransom money."

"You think Zirkon will really show up?" asked the President. "I really have to get my human body back tonight."

"He may come by helicopter, or even by blimp," I whispered. "But he'll be here, all

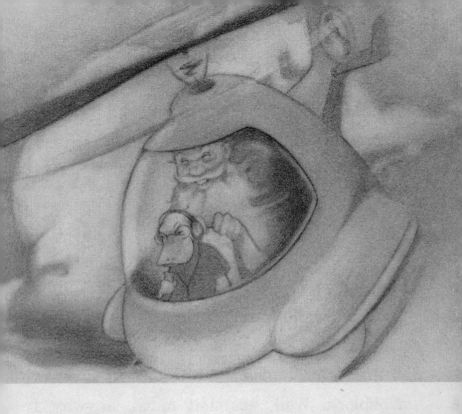

right. He wants that money as much as you
want your body back."

"OK, Max," said the President.

I crept around the corner of the building. I hid so that nobody who was with the
President could see me, but I could see
them. I waited.

Soon, Dr. Zirkon would appear. Dr. Zirkon, the evil scientist who had turned into a duck-billed platypus when an experiment he was doing went terribly wrong. He'd be with his assistant, Nobblock. Nobblock, the crazed serial killer and former wrestler he helped escape from prison. The maniac who once bit the head off an alligator and swallowed it whole.

I looked at my watch. It was eight-forty-five. I wasn't afraid of Zirkon, or even of Nobblock. Well, not that much, anyway. I mean, Nobblock was a grown-up serial killer, and Zirkon was a grown-up duck-billed platypus. I was just an eleven-year-old boy, but my superpowers protected me.

I looked at my watch again. Almost nine o'clock. Was Zirkon coming or wasn't he?

"Pssst!" The sound was right behind me.

I spun around to see . . . Pete Delete! He was still wearing his ratty bathrobe and bunny slippers. He was carrying his Mind-Eraser.

"Delete," I said. "What the heck are *you* doing here?"

Delete smiled.

"What number can you add to ten, or subtract from twenty, and get the same answer?" he asked me.

Oh, no! A math problem! I got dizzy. I sank to my knees. I almost blacked out. I was completely helpless.

What terrible luck to have this idiot Delete ask me a math problem at a time like this! At a time when Zirkon and Nobblock would be showing up any second now! How could I protect the President? How could I protect *myself*? Well, it wasn't Delete's fault. He couldn't have known that even *hearing* a math problem would paralyze me. Or could he?

And then, suddenly, horribly, I realized the truth. It wasn't Zirkon and Nobblock I had to worry about. It wasn't them at all.

"It wasn't *Zirkon* who turned the President into a chimp," I said weakly. "It was *you*, wasn't it?"

CHAPTER 12

"Zirkon!" sneered Delete. "Of *course* it wasn't Zirkon. Zirkon is a fool! Zirkon turned himself into a platypus because he didn't understand his own invention." Delete held up his black box. "Fortunately, I understand mine."

"The Mind-Eraser," I said.

"This is a lot more than a Mind-Eraser,"

said Delete. "This is what turned the President into a chimp. Soon it will turn *you* into a cockroach!"

Oh, boy, did I ever not want to be turned into a cockroach! I had enough problems just being an eleven-year-old boy. Of course, cockroaches didn't have to go to school. . . .

"I thought in order to turn somebody into an animal you had to have a beam focused on both the person and the animal," I said. "Then you switched signals and teleported each to the other's body."

"That's not how I do it at all," said Delete. "Who told you that's how I do it?"

"Tortoise Man."

"Tortoise Man is a fool!" said Delete. "All superheroes are fools!"

The effects of the math problem were beginning to wear off. If I could just keep him talking a little longer, I might regain my strength.

"If all superheroes are fools, Delete, then why do you help them?" I asked. "Why do you erase the minds of people who find out their secret identities?"

"Why?" said Delete. "To get them to do me favors. Like fixing my air conditioner. Certainly not because I *like* them."

"And why did you turn the President into a chimp?"

"Because *he* made a monkey out of *me*."

"What do you mean?"

"I was not always as you see me now. I was once an important scientist in a government lab. *Dr.* Pete Delete."

"What were you working on?"

"A secret weapon for the army to turn enemy soldiers into jungle animals. As soon as he got elected, this President canceled our project and fired everyone who worked on it, including me. I lost everything. That's when I decided to make a monkey out of him and get paid for it. OK, enough talk. Where's my money?"

"Delete, don't take the money," I said. "Just turn the President back into a human. I don't think it's illegal to turn Presidents into chimps. If you don't take the money, you haven't broken any laws and you can go free. What do you say?"

Delete seemed to be thinking it over.

"No," he said, "I want my money. Where is it?"

I sighed and shook my head.

"The money is here," I said. "But first, turn the President back into a human."

"How do I know you'll give me the money afterward?"

"If I don't, you can always turn him back into a chimp again," I said.

"Or turn *you* into a cockroach," he said.

"Uh, right."

"OK," said Delete. "Call him. Call the President."

"Mr. President?" I called out. "Come on over here! You're about to be turned back into a human!"

The chimp came cautiously around the corner of the balcony and saw Delete.

"This isn't Dr. Zirkon," he said.

"No," said Delete, "it certainly isn't."

"Sir, this is Dr. Pete Delete," I said. "The man who changed you into a chimp. He's now going to change you back into a man."

"On second thought," said Delete, "I don't trust you. I want my money first."

I looked upward. I saw what I hoped I'd see.

"OK, Delete," I said. "Whatever you say."

"Where *is* my money?" Delete demanded.

"Where is Dr. Delete's money?" I shouted. I had almost all my strength back.

"It's up here, Delete!" came a voice from above our heads.

Delete looked up.

Sitting 230 feet above the one-hundred-and-second-floor balcony, on the very tip of the antenna at the top of the Empire State Building, was Tiffany. Just as we had planned, she was holding onto a gigantic sack. It must have weighed a ton or more. She could never have held onto it without superpowers. But, knowing how clumsy she was, she might drop it at any second. I prayed she wouldn't drop it.

"Here's your money, Delete!" she shouted. "Unfortunately, it's all in pennies. I'll just drop it down on you so you can count it!"

Delete realized we had him.

"No!" he screamed. "You can't do that!"

"Yes, she can," I said. "If it doesn't flatten you on the balcony, it'll knock you over the railing. Your trip down to the street will do the same thing."

"No!" screamed Delete. "Don't drop it! Please!"

"Then turn on your machine," I said. "And if the President doesn't come out perfect, you'll be flatter than a flapjack at the International House of Pancakes."

Delete turned on his black box and aimed it at the President. He pressed three buttons. He pushed four toggle switches. The machine crackled and whirred.

A strange blue glow surrounded the chimp. Within the blue glow, the chimp began to grow. And grow. And grow. His clothes split and fell off. The President was human again. And stark naked.

I quickly tore off Delete's filthy robe and wrapped it around the naked President.

"Thanks, Max," said the President.

"You're welcome, sir," I said.

"Hey, what about *me*?" cried Delete.

I probably shouldn't have cared about Delete, but he looked so pitiful, standing there in his underwear and bunny slippers. I threw him what was left of the chimp's little suit. It was almost big enough to fit him. But first I took away his black box.

"OK, Tiffany," I called. "You can fly that sack of pennies down to the street!"

I was amazed and relieved she had done everything I told her to without screwing up. I turned to Delete.

"Pete Delete," I said, "by the powers vested in me by the League of Superheroes. of the United States of America, I hereby arrest you."

"If you divide a number by two and then add one . . ." Delete began.

But before he could finish his sentence, I knocked him out cold.

So we flew Delete to jail, and then we flew the President in his human body back to Washington. He was grateful and thanked us all over the place. We even got back home to Chicago around ten o'clock, so Mom and Dad weren't too freaked out.

Oh, yeah. The President's speech Thursday night went off OK. He even thanked me and Tiffany on national TV. He didn't use our real names, of course.

So everything got back to normal again.

Then, one Saturday morning, something happened that put not only me and Tiffany in the worst danger of our lives, but it threatened all the people on Earth!

**Check out this sneak
preview from the next
nail-biting Maximum Boy Adventure!**

ATTACK OF THE SOGGY UNDERWATER PEOPLE

Suddenly, there was movement among the creatures. The biggest one took a step forward. He seemed to be their leader. Flaps extended all around his mouth, just like a megaphone. He began to speak. His voice was loud and kind of gurgly. It sounded like he was speaking through water.

"Grrreetings, Drrrylanderrrs!" he said.

"We arrrre the Waterrr People. We have come to take overrr yourrr worrrld."

"Uh-oh," said the cop. "That doesn't sound good."

"Who among you speaks forrr the Drrrylanderrrs?" asked the creature.

None of the cops or news reporters said a word.

"Who speaks forrr the Drrryland-errrs?!!" shouted the creature.

I realized it was probably me who had to answer. My heart started hammering in my chest. I was pretty scared, but I stepped forward. I could hardly breathe.

"*I* s-s-speak for the D-d-drylanders," I said.

"M-me, too," said Tiffany, but so quietly not even the cops heard her.

The creature stretched its neck forward to look at me. Its neck extended at least five feet. Then it burst into horrible sounds that sounded like gurgly laughter. The other creatures started laughing, too.

"*You* speak for the Drrrylanderrrs?" roared the creature. "But you arrre a *baby*."

That got me mad.

"A baby?" I said. "I am not a *baby*! I'm eleven and a half!"

The creature roared with more of its terrible laughter. So did the others. These things were not only ugly, they were rude. The creatures slowly got over their laughter.

"Since the little baby is the only Drrry-landerrr brrrave enough to speak to us," it said, "I will speak to the little baby."

"Thanks a lot," I said sarcastically. "Thanks for *nothing*." I was pretty angry, but I remembered I was here on official business. "Where are you from, Atlantis?"

That started more nasty laughter.

"Atlantis is but a small parrrt of ourrr underrrwaterrr worrrld. Saying all Waterrr People arrre from Atlantis is like saying all Drrrylanderrrs arrre frrrom Cleveland."

The creatures laughed some more.

"No, little baby, we arrre the Waterrr People. The Waterrr People live in all oceans, deep lakes, and rrriverrrs. Pitiful Drrrylanderrrs, this planet is ninety percent waterrr. We have generrrously allowed you to sharrre the planet, and what do you do? You pollute it. Yourrr tankerrr ships spill millions of gallons of oil into ourrr oceans. Yourrr factorrries spill toxic chemicals into our rrriverrrs. When you go swimming, you pee in ourrr water — in the waterrr we *brrreathe*. Well, we'rrre fed up and we'rrre not going to take it any longerrr!"

"Excuse me," I interrupted, "but Earth isn't ninety percent water, it's around seventy-five percent. We studied that in school."

"It *is* ninety percent, little baby, if you include rrriverrrs, lakes, aquarrriums, swimming pools, and toilets. Who is the leaderrr of all the Drrrylanderrrs? I wish to speak to him."

"The leader of this particular country is the President of the United States," I said.

"Then tell the Prrresident *this*, little baby: The Waterrr People have come to take overrr the Drrrylanderrrs and the Drrry Worrrld! Unless you surrrenderrr, we shall unleash upon all nations of the Drrry Worrrld devastating floods and tidal waves!

We shall sink you! We shall drrrown you and drrrain you of your verrry last airrr bubble!"

"Yeah?" I said. "Well, we're not afraid of you."

"Pitiful Drrrylanderrrs!" shrieked the creature. "You are no match forrr the Waterrr People! We declarrre warrr on all Drrrylanderrrs, starrrting Thurrrsday! We wanted to make it Tuesday, but I had a dentist appointment."

"Thursday is fine with *us*!" I shouted.

ABOUT THE AUTHOR

When he was a kid, author Dan Greenburg used to be a lot like Maximum Boy — he lived with his parents and sister in Chicago, he was skinny, he wore glasses and braces, he was a lousy athlete, he was allergic to milk products, and he became dizzy when exposed to math problems. Unlike Maximum Boy, Dan was never able to lift locomotives or fly.

As an adult, Dan has written more than forty books for both kids and grown-ups, which have been reprinted in twenty-three countries. His kids' books include the series The Zack Files, which is also a TV series. His grown-up books include *How to Be a Jewish Mother* and *How to Make Yourself Miserable*. Dan has written for the movies and TV, the Broadway stage, and most national magazines. He has appeared on network TV as an author and comedian. He is still trying to lift locomotives and fly.

WATCH YOUR BACK!

Visit Captain Underpants online and play the Wedgie Woman Game!

www.scholastic.com/ captainunderpants